DOCTOR DOLITTLE

SAVES THE DAY

A Red Fox Book

Published by Random House Children's Books
20 Vauxhall Bridge Road, London SW1V 2SA

A division of The Random House Group Ltd
London Melbourne Sydney Auckland
Johannesburg and agencies throughout the world

Copyright © Christopher Lofting 1999

Text abridged from *Doctor Dolittle's Zoo*
Copyright, 1926, by Hugh Lofting
Copyright © Christopher Lofting 1992

1 3 5 7 9 10 8 6 4 2

This Junior Novel first published in Great Britain
by Red Fox 2000

Printed and bound in Denmark by
Nørhaven A/S, Viborg

Papers used by The Random House Group Limited are natural, recyclable products
made from wood grownin sustainable forests. The manufacturing processes
conform to the environmental regulations of the country of origin.

THE RANDOM HOUSE GROUP Limited Reg. No. 954009

ISBN 0 09 940604 7

DOCTOR DOLITTLE

SAVES THE DAY

From the stories by
HUGH LOFTING

Abridged by
CHARLIE SHEPPARD

RED FOX

For
Helena Sheppard

1. *Where to Begin*

'Polynesia,' I said, leaning back in my chair and chewing the end of my pen, 'what do you think would be the best way to begin another book of Doctor Dolittle's adventures?'

The old parrot, who was using the glass inkpot on my desk as a mirror, stopped admiring her reflection and glanced at me sharply. 'Tommy Stubbins,' she said, screwing up her eyes, 'that's a very difficult question to answer. There is so much of interest in the life of John Dolittle that if you try to write down everything he did, you'll be nearly my age before you've finished. Mind you, I often wonder why you don't write a natural history

book, seeing as you're the only person so far —
besides the Doctor — who can actually talk
to animals.'

'Well that's because I was lucky enough to be
his assistant for all those years,' I said.

'True indeed. Anyway, I suppose a highbrow
book can come later. The life of Doctor Dolittle
is *far* more important. But how to begin.
Humph! Well why not go on from where we
discovered the fire at Moorsden Manor.'

'Yes,' I said. 'I thought of beginning there.
But it was more *how* than where — I mean, the
things to leave out and the things to put in;
what parts to choose as the most interesting.'

Polynesia thought for a moment. 'What are
you calling the book?' she asked.

'*Doctor Dolittle Saves the Day*,' I said.

'Humph!' she murmured. 'An excellent title.
Then I suppose you must just write about the
day he saved as soon as possible.'

'I suppose I must.'

'Well,' continued Polynesia. 'I think it would
be best if you read it all out aloud to me as you
put it down; and if it starts to get boring you'll
know, because you'll see me dropping off to sleep.

You will have to keep it bright and lively though, because as I get older I find it harder and harder to stay awake after lunch. Have you got enough paper? Yes. And the inkpot is full? Yes. All right. Get along with it.'

So carefully picking up my pen and dipping it in the ink, I began:

I suppose there is no part of my life that I, Tommy Stubbins, look back on with more pleasure than the time I lived with the incredible Doctor Dolittle and worked as his assistant.

I had joined the Doctor several years before as a young boy and had been taught by him and Polynesia to speak a few animal languages. We lived happily in the Doctor's house in Puddleby-on-the-Marsh along with some other animals who were all part of Doctor Dolittle's big family.

There was Dab-Dab the duck, who was housekeeper to the Doctor. She cooked and cleaned for the Doctor and his strange animal family. Too-Too the owl was an excellent mathematician and looked after the Doctor's money. Jip the dog was a great friend to the Doctor and whenever a job of scenting or detecting needed to be done, he had no equal.

But these weren't the only animal friends who lived with us. Gub-Gub the pig, Whitey the white mouse and Chee-Chee the monkey were also members of our happy household.

Doctor Dolittle was always kind and pleasant to everyone but he much preferred the company of animals. Ever since he'd decided to stop being a people's doctor and become an animal doctor, he'd spent less and less time with his neighbours. There was one man in Puddleby, however, who had always been a good friend to the Doctor, and always seemed to be around whenever there was an adventure to be had, and that was Matthew Mugg, the Cats'-meat-man.

The only other human living in Doctor Dolittle's house during our Moorsden Manor adventure was Bumpo, the African prince whom we had met on our travels. Bumpo was on holiday in Puddleby and staying with the Doctor. He was a good friend to us all and we always looked forward to his visits.

2. Fire! Fire!

One evening the Doctor and I were sitting up discussing a difficult case of a broken wing we'd seen that day. It was late and Bumpo, who had been yawning for the past hour, had finally gone to bed. Dab-Dab was making some cocoa at the stove, and Gub-Gub was snoozing by the fire, dreaming of a delicious turnip.

Suddenly there was a scratching at the door and Whitey, the white mouse, burst in. 'Sorry to disturb you, Doctor,' he said, 'but there's a mouse here from Moorsden Manor. He says he really must see you, it's important.'

Before the Doctor could answer, a breathless mouse pushed past Whitey and raced towards me and the Doctor.

'Doctor,' he cried, 'there's a fire over at Moorsden Manor. It's in the cellar. And everybody's sleeping and no one knows anything about it.'

'Good gracious!' cried the Doctor, standing up and looking at his watch. 'Asleep! Is it as late as that? Why, so it is. What's in the cellar – wood, coal?'

'It's full of wood,' said the mouse. 'But the fire hasn't got to it yet – thank goodness! My nest, with five babies in it, is right in the middle of the woodpile. The wife thought the best thing I could do would be to come and tell you. Nobody else understands our language, anyway. She's staying with the children. The fire started in a heap of old sacks lying in a corner of the cellar. The place is full of smoke already. There is no chance of our carrying the babies out because there are too many cats about. Once the fire reaches the wood it's all up with us. Won't you come – quickly, Doctor?'

'Of course I will,' said John Dolittle. 'Stubbins,' he called to me, 'go and wake Bumpo – and send Jip along to Matthew's house. We'd better get all the help we can. If the blaze hasn't gone too far we can probably get it under control. Here's a note that Jip can give to Matthew, for the fire brigade – but it always takes them a long time to get on the scene.'

He hastily scribbled a few words on an old envelope, with which I dashed off in one direction, while he disappeared in another.

For the next fifteen minutes I was busy trying

to get Jip and Bumpo up and telling them about the fire. Bumpo was always the slowest man in the world to wake up. But after a good deal of hard work I managed to get him interested in clothes – and fires. Jip, I had already sent trotting down the Oxenthorpe Road with his note to fetch Matthew to the scene.

Then I clutched Bumpo (still only half dressed and half awake) firmly by the hand and hurried off after the Doctor in the direction of the fire.

Now Moorsden Manor was the largest house in Puddleby. Like the Doctor's home, it was on the outskirts of the town and was surrounded by a large piece of land. Its owner, Mr Sidney Throgmorton, was a middle-aged man who had only recently inherited the property. His millionaire father had died the year before, leaving him this and several other big estates in England and Scotland. And many people were surprised that he remained at the Manor all the year round when he had so many other castles and fine houses to go to.

The main gates to the estate were guarded by a lodge. And when I arrived I found the Doctor hammering on the door trying to wake up the lodgekeeper. The gates, of course, were locked; and the whole of the grounds were enclosed by a wall which was much too high to climb over.

Almost at the same moment that Bumpo and I got there, Matthew Mugg, led by Jip, also arrived.

'Good gracious!' the Doctor was saying as he thumped the door with his fist. 'What sleepers! The whole place could burn down while we're standing here. Do you think the lodge is empty?'

'No,' said Matthew. 'The keeper's here – or his wife. One of them is always on duty. I'll throw a stone against the window.'

It was only a small pebble that he threw, but the Cats'-meat-man put such force behind it that it went right through the glass with a crash.

Angry shouts from inside told us that at last we had managed to wake someone up. And a few moments later a man in a nightshirt, with a shotgun in one hand and a candle in the other, appeared at the door. As the Doctor stepped forward he quickly put the candle down and raised the gun as if to shoot.

'It's all right,' said John Dolittle. 'I've only come to warn you. There's a fire up at the Manor – in the cellar. The people must be warned at once. Let me through, please.'

'I will not let you through,' said the man stubbornly. 'I've heard about hold-up gangs playing that trick before. The cheek of you, coming breaking my windows at this time of night! And how do you know what's going on up at the Manor?'

'A mouse told me,' said the Doctor. Then seeing the look of disbelief on the man's face, he added, 'Oh, don't argue with me! I know there's a fire there. Please just let us in?'

But the man had no intention of doing so. And I cannot say that he should be altogether blamed for that. For we certainly must have seemed a strange group to call in the middle of the night.

Goodness only knows how long we would have stood there while the fire in the Manor cellar went on growing, if Matthew hadn't decided to deal with the situation in his own peculiar way. With a whispered word to Bumpo he suddenly ducked forward and wrenched the shotgun out of the lodge-keeper's hands. Bumpo grabbed the candle that stood beside the door. And the fort was in our possession.

'Come on, Doctor,' said Matthew. 'There's another door through here which leads into the grounds. We can't wait to talk things over with him. Maybe when the fire brigade gets here he will believe that there really is a fire.'

Bumpo had already found and opened the second door. And before the astonished keeper had had time to get his breath we were all through it and running up the drive that led to the big house.

'I suppose it will take us another age to get anyone awake here,' gasped the Doctor as we arrived breathless and gazed up the high double doors.

'No, it won't,' said Matthew. And he let off the lodge-keeper's shotgun at the stars and started yelling 'Fire!' at the top of his voice.

The Doctor, Bumpo and I added to the noise by hammering on the panels and calling loudly for someone to let us in.

But we did not have long to wait this time. The shotgun was a good alarm. Almost immediately lights appeared in various parts of the house. Next, several windows were thrown open and heads popped out demanding to know what was the matter.

'There's a fire,' the Doctor shouted. 'A fire in your house! Open the doors and let us in.'

A few minutes later the heavy bolts were shot back and an old servant with a candle opened the door.

'I can't find the master,' he said to the Doctor. 'He isn't in his room. He must have fallen asleep in some other part of the house. All the rest have been woken up. But I can't find the master.'

'Where's the cellar?' asked the Doctor, taking the candle and hurrying by him. 'Show me the way to the cellar.'

But the master wouldn't be in the cellar, sir,' said the old man. 'What do you want in the cellar?'

'A family of mice,' said the Doctor, 'young ones. They're in great danger. Their nest is in the woodpile. Show me the way, quickly!'

3. Safe at Last

I think that, for both the Doctor and myself, that was one of the most extraordinary nights we ever experienced. When Matthew, Bumpo and I followed Doctor Dolittle into the hall of the great house we found things in a pretty wild state of confusion. In various stages of dress and undress people were running up and down stairs, dragging trunks, throwing valuables over the banisters and generally behaving like a hen-roost in a panic. The smell of smoke was very strong; and when more candles had been lit I could see that the hall was partly filled with it.

There was no need for the Doctor now to ask the way to the cellar. Over to the left of the

hall there was a door leading downward by an old-fashioned winding stair. And through it the smoke was pouring upwards at a terrible rate.

To my horror, the Doctor tied a handkerchief about his face, dashed through this doorway and disappeared into the screen of smoke before anyone had time to stop him. Seeing that Bumpo and I had it in our minds to follow, Matthew held out his hand.

'Don't. You'd be more trouble than help to him,' he said. 'If you were overcome, the Doctor would have to fetch you up too. Let's get outside and break the cellar windows. It must be full of smoke down there – more smoke than fire, most likely. If we can let some of it out, maybe the Doctor can see what he's doing.'

With that all three of us ran for the front door. On the way we bumped into the old servant, who was still wandering aimlessly around, wringing his hands and wailing that he couldn't find 'the master'. Matthew grabbed him and shoved him along ahead of us into the front garden.

'Now,' he said, 'where are the cellar windows? Quick, lead us to 'em!'

Well, finally we got the poor old doddering butler to take us to the back of the house where, on either side of the kitchen door, there were two cellar windows. To his great astonishment and horror we promptly proceeded to kick the glass out of them. Heavy choking smoke immediately belched into our faces.

'Hulloa there! Doctor!' gasped Matthew. 'Are you all right?'

The Cats'-meat-man had brought a lantern with him. He shone it down into the reeking blackness of the cellar. For a few moments, which seemed eternally long, I was in an agony of suspense waiting for the answering shout that didn't come. Matthew glanced upwards over his shoulder.

'Humph!' he grunted with a frown. 'Looks as though we'll have to organize a rescue party.'

But just as he was about to set off for help I clutched him by the arm.

'Look!' I said, pointing downwards.

And there in the beam of his lantern a hand could be seen coming through the smoking hole in the broken window. It was the Doctor's hand. And in the hollow of the half-open palm, five pink and hairless baby mice were nestling.

'Well, I'll be blowed!' muttered Matthew, taking the family and passing them up to me.

The Doctor's hand withdrew and almost immediately reappeared again, this time with the thoroughly frightened mother-mouse – whom I also pocketed.

But Matthew didn't wait for the Doctor's hand to go back for anything else. He grabbed it

by the wrist and with a mighty heave pulled
John Dolittle, with the window-sash and all, up
into the open air. We saw at once that he was
staggering and in pretty bad condition, and we
dragged him away from the choking smoke, to
a lawn near by. Here we stretched him out flat
and undid his collar.

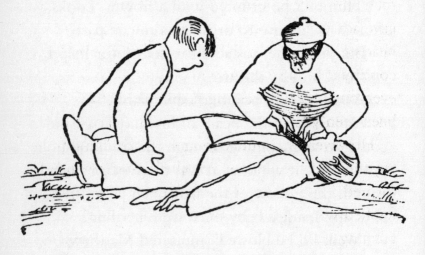

But before we had time to do anything else
for him he began to struggle to his feet.

'I'm all right,' he gasped. 'It was only the
smoke. We must get a bucket chain started.
The fire has just reached the woodpile. If it's
allowed to get a good hold the whole place
will burn down.'

There is not the least doubt that that mouse who brought the news of the fire to the Doctor saved Moorsden Manor from total destruction – and possibly several lives as well. Certainly if it had not been for our efforts the place would never have been saved by those living there, even if they had woken up in time. I never saw such an hysterical crew in my life. Everybody gave advice and nobody did anything. And the head of the servants, the old white-haired butler, continued to dodder around getting in everyone's way, still asking if the master had been seen yet.

However, without waiting for assistance from anyone else, the Doctor, Matthew, Bumpo and I formed a bucket line on our own, and by it we fetched water from the kitchen sink to the burning sacks and firewood. And soon nothing remained of what had promised to be a very serious fire but a charred and hissing mass.

In addition to this Matthew discovered a tap in the garden and, with the help of a hose which we found in the stable, we brought another stream of water to the cellar through the broken window.

While we were attaching the hose in the
garden a man suddenly appeared out of a
shrubbery and shouted at the Doctor in a very
unfriendly manner.

'Who are you?'

'I?' said the Doctor, a little taken aback. 'I'm
John Dolittle. Er – and you?'

'My name is Sidney Throgmorton,' said the
man. 'And I would like to know what you
mean by breaking into my lodge at this hour
of night, smashing windows and assaulting
the keeper.'

'Why, good gracious!' said the Doctor. 'We wanted to warn you about the fire. We hadn't got time to wait around. The keeper wouldn't let us in. As it was, we only just got here in time. I think I can assure you that if we hadn't got here the house would have been burned to the ground.'

I now saw in the gloom behind the man's shoulder that the lodge-keeper was with him.

'You have acted in a very high-handed manner, sir,' said Sidney Throgmorton. 'My lodge-keeper has his orders as to who can, and who cannot, come in. And there is a fire department in the town whose business it is to look after fires. For you to barge your way into my home in this violent manner is nothing short of a scandal, sir – for which I have a good mind to have you arrested. I will ask you and your friends to leave my premises at once.'

4. The Leather Boxes

For a moment or two the Doctor was clearly about to reply. I could see by the dim light of Matthew's lantern the anger in his face. But finally he seemed to decide it was no good talking to a man like this.

'My coat is in your cellar,' said the Doctor quietly at last. 'I will get it. Then we will go.'

To add insult to injury, the man actually followed us down into the cellar, as though we might steal something if we were not watched. The man muttered angrily under his breath when he saw the water which flooded the floor.

At this last show of ingratitude for what we had done, Bumpo could contain his anger no longer.

'Why you rude and worm-like boor!' he began, advancing upon Throgmorton with battle in his eye.

'Please! Bumpo!' the Doctor interrupted. 'No further words are necessary. We will go.'

By the brighter light of the lamps I now saw that Throgmorton carried beneath his arm several small leather boxes. In climbing up over the woodpile, in order to see what damage we might have done on the other side, he laid these down for a moment on top of a wine cask.

I was close to Matthew. In the fraction of a second, while Throgmorton's back was turned, I saw the Cats'-meat-man open the top one of the boxes, glance into it and shut it again.

The box contained four enormous diamond shirt-studs.

As soon as he had his coat the Doctor wasted no further time, but made his way, with us following him, up the stairs and out of the house which he had saved from destruction.

The keeper took us to the lodge and let us out. Matthew, like Bumpo, was just burning to speak his mind, but the Doctor seemed determined that there should be no further trouble and stopped Matthew every time he tried to open his mouth.

However, at the gate we met the fire brigade coming to the rescue. This was too much for Matthew's self-control, and he called to them as we stepped out on to the road: 'Oh, turn around and go back to bed! We put that fire out before you'd got your boots on.'

Outside the boundaries of the Moorsden Manor estate not even the Doctor could stop Matthew's and Bumpo's anger.

'Well, of all the good-for-nothing, mangy, low-down ungrateful . . .' the Cats'-meat-man began, 'that stuffed pillow of a millionaire takes the prize! After all we've done for him! Getting up out of our beds, working like horses – all to keep his bloomin' mansion from burning down.

And then he tells us we've ruined his cellar by pouring water into it!'

'It was only with the greatest difficulty that I restrained myself from hitting him on the nose,' said Bumpo.

'Enough,' said the Doctor. 'Please don't say any more. I am trying to forget it. The whole affair is just one of those incidents which it is no use thinking about or getting yourself worked up over afterwards. I'm often very grateful that life has made it possible for me to keep away from my neighbours and mind my own business. This situation couldn't be helped – but it has made me even more grateful. Thank goodness, anyway, that we got the mice out all right before the fire reached them. You've got them safely in your pocket, Stubbins, haven't you?'

'Yes,' I said, putting my hand in to make sure. 'Oh, but, Doctor, your hat? Where is it? You've left it behind.'

John Dolittle raised his hand to his bare head.

'Dear me!' he said. 'What a nuisance! Well, I'll have to go back, that's all.'

I knew how he hated to. But the well-loved

hat was too precious to leave behind. In silence all four of us turned about.

The gate was still open from the arrival of the fire brigade. Unchallenged, we walked in and down the drive towards the house.

Halfway along, the Doctor paused.

'Perhaps it would be better,' he said, 'if you waited here for me. After all, there is no need for four of us to fetch a hat.'

He went on alone while we stood in the shadow of the trees. The moon had now risen and we could see more clearly.

I noticed that Matthew was restless and fidgety. He kept muttering to himself and peering after the Doctor down the drive. Eventually in a determined whisper he said: 'No. I'm blessed if I'll let him go alone! I don't trust that Mr Throgmorton. Come on, you chaps. Let's follow the Doctor. Keep low, behind the trees. Don't let yourselves be seen. I suspect he might need us.'

I had no idea what was in Matthew's mind. But from experience I knew that usually when he acted on impulse like this, he acted rightly. So like a band of Indian scouts, scuttling from tree to tree, we followed the Doctor up the drive till he came to the clearing before the house.

Here the fire brigade, with a great deal of bother and fuss, was about to leave – after its captain had made sure that the fire was really out. The big door lamps had been lit and the courtyard was fairly well illuminated. Mr Throgmorton could be seen talking to the firemen. We saw John Dolittle go up to him, but Mr Throgmorton pretended to be too busy to notice anything but the fire brigade.

And it was only after the engine had clattered noisily away that Mr Throgmorton bothered to notice John Dolittle. This time he did not wait for the Doctor to speak.

'You here again!' he shouted. 'Didn't I tell you to get off the premises? Clear out of here, or I'll set the dogs on you.'

'I've come back for my hat,' said the Doctor, controlling himself. 'It's in the hall.'

'Get out of here!' the other repeated threateningly. 'I'll have no more of you suspicious characters messing round my place tonight. I find you smashed the windows in the cellar as well as the lodge. Clear out, unless you want the dogs after you.'

'I will not go,' said the Doctor firmly, 'until I have my hat.'

('My goodness! But I'd love to give that fellow a crack on the jaw!' whispered Matthew, who was standing next to me.)

The Doctor's answer seemed to infuriate Throgmorton even more. He drew a whistle from his pocket and blew upon it loudly. An answering shout came from somewhere in the darkness of the gardens.

'Let go Dina and Wolf!' called Throgmorton.

(That's his two man-killing mastiffs,' chuckled Matthew in my ear. 'I know 'em – regular savages. He keeps 'em to defend the place. Now we'll see some fun.')

5. The Watch Dogs

Next moment we heard a scraping rush of paws upon the gravel and two gigantic dogs bounded out of the gloom into the courtyard.

'Grab 'im! Go get 'im!' shouted Throgmorton.

Together the two dogs hurled themselves towards the figure of the stranger. Then Mr Throgmorton got a big surprise. The stranger did not run or indeed show any panic whatever. But as he turned his face in the direction of the oncoming dogs he made some curious sounds, almost like another kind of growl answering theirs.

At this the two hounds behaved in a most curious manner. Instead of grasping their prey by the throat, they wagged their tails, licked his hand and generally carried on as though he were no stranger at all, but a very old and dear friend of theirs. Then, in response to an order he gave them, they disappeared into the darkness from which they had come.

Beside me, behind the tree, Matthew covered his face with his hand to stop himself laughing. 'Good old Doctor Dolittle,' he said. 'Mr Throgmorton should know better than to mess with the only man who can talk to animals.'

'I will now get my hat,' said the Doctor. And he walked calmly into the house.

Mr Throgmorton was just speechless with rage. To be made to look ridiculous like this by such a quiet small person was more than he could bear.

Within the hall the Doctor could now be seen on his way out – with the precious hat. Throgmorton hid in the shadow of a door-column and waited.

'Yes, I thought so!' muttered Matthew. And he slid like a shadow out from behind the tree and crept towards the waiting figure of Throgmorton.

John Dolittle, unaware of anything except the fact that he was anxious to get away from this horrible house as soon as possible, stepped briskly forward on to the gravel. An enormous weight landed on his shoulders and pinned him to the ground.

'I'll teach you,' growled Throgmorton, 'to walk in and out of my house as though you–'

But he got no further, for Matthew had landed on top of him just as *he* had landed on the Doctor.

But Sidney Throgmorton, in spite of his fat, unhealthy appearance, was a heavy, powerful man. He rose and threw Matthew off as though he were a fly. And he was just about to aim a kick at the Doctor lying on the ground when he suddenly found himself gripped from behind and lifted off his feet like a doll.

Indeed Bumpo not only lifted him, but was now carrying his fat victim bodily away towards the Manor.

'Well!' said the Doctor, rising and brushing his clothes, 'what an offensive person! Who would ever have thought he'd do that! The man must be out of his senses.'

'I'll have you all in jail for this,' grunted Throgmorton, as Bumpo let him fall heavily, like a large sack of potatoes, to the ground.

'If you take my advice,' grinned Matthew, 'you'll keep your silly mouth shut. There's three witnesses here saw you make that attack on the Doctor – slinking up and waiting for him behind the door-post. And don't forget, his honesty is as well known as yours you know – maybe better. Your money can't do everything.'

'And I have witnesses too,' spluttered Mr Throgmorton, 'who saw you all breaking into my lodge and using violence on the keeper.'

'Yes, to save your hide and your house from burning,' added Matthew. 'Go on and do your worst. I dare you to take it to any court.'

'Come, come!' said the Doctor, herding us away like children. 'Let us be going. No more, Matthew – please! Come, Bumpo!'

And leaving the fuming, spluttering master of the Manor to pick himself up from the gravel, we walked down the drive.

During the walk home all four of us were silent – also a little tired, for, as Matthew had said, we had worked hard at our thankless task. And we must have been more than halfway to the house before anyone spoke. It was the Cats'-meat-man.

'You know,' he said, breaking out suddenly, 'there's something fishy about the whole thing. That's my opinion.'

'How do you mean?' said the Doctor sleepily, trying to show polite interest.

'About his ingratitude,' said Matthew, 'his wanting to get us off the place in such a hurry and – and, well, his general manner. I don't believe he ever thought we were suspicious characters at all – maybe the lodge-keeper might have, but not the owner. Why, everyone in Puddleby knows you, Doctor . . . And then the way things was run, up at the house there: nobody in charge unless the "master" is on the job. And the master wasn't . . . Why wasn't he? What was he doing all the time while old Moses was running round hollering for him? . . . And why–'

'Oh, Matthew,' the Doctor broke in, 'what's the use of guessing and speculating about it? Personally, I don't care what he was doing – or what he ever will do. Thank goodness, the whole stupid affair is over!'

But Matthew was much too wrapped up in his subject to dismiss it like that. And though he kept his voice low, as if he were talking to himself, he continued a one-man conversation for the rest of the way home.

'Yes, there's a mystery there, all right. And if anybody was to get to the bottom of it I'll bet they'd get a shock . . . Why, even the lodge-keeper – there's another queer thing: supposing he *was* scared by the way we woke him up, just the same, no man in his senses – orders or no orders – is going to take no notice of a fire alarm. If he didn't want to let us in, he could always call to his wife and send her up to the

Manor to find out. And then when he does
follow us up to the house, and sees that there
really is a fire, does he do anything to help us put
it out? No, he does not. He goes and tells the
precious "master" how badly we treated him
getting in to save them all from burning to death.
And, by the way, that's still another queer thing:
how did he know where to find the master? The
old butler didn't know – no, nor nobody else.'

The Doctor sighed gratefully as we finally reached the little gate. After this hard and trying night the thought of a good bed was very pleasant – as was also the prospect of getting some peace from Matthew's thinking aloud.

6. The Scrap of Parchment

The rescued mouse family, which I had brought home in my pocket, were given a place to stay in Doctor Dolittle's house. Whitey personally saw to it that they were made comfortable. And, of course, they immediately became heroes in the household. The thrilling story they had to tell of the fire; the father-mouse's midnight gallop for help; their rescue by John Dolittle himself; and finally the Doctor's treatment at the hands of Mr Throgmorton, was told again and again to everyone's delight.

When other mice in the area heard of how badly the Doctor had been treated they wanted to organize a campaign of revenge – which would, I believe, have utterly ruined the Manor if they had been allowed to carry it out. For they planned to chew up the curtains, drill the panelling, eat holes in the tapestries, break the wine glasses, and a whole lot of other mischief which mice can easily do if they want to. But to their frustration, as to Matthew's, the Doctor turned a deaf ear. He wanted to forget the whole incident.

Nevertheless, the local mice continued to discuss Mr Throgmorton's behaviour towards the Doctor, and any mice from the Manor who dropped in to see the mouse family were always the centre of attention while they stayed, so great was everyone's interest in gossip from the big house.

And it was through this that the poor Doctor, despite his desire to stay away from Sidney Throgmorton, found himself forced to take a further part in the matters which he insisted were 'none of his business'.

It began by Whitey coming to me one night and saying: 'There's a mouse just run over from the Manor who has lived up there for some time. He has something he wants to show the

Doctor. But the poor man is always so busy I thought I'd speak to you first. Will you come and see him?'

'All right,' I said. And I left what I was doing and went down right away.

When I got downstairs I found a mouse surrounded by other local rodents. They were all staring at a torn scrap of paper about the size of a business card.

'I thought this might be of importance,' said the mouse to me. 'Of course I can't read what it says on it. But it is made of a very special kind of paper. That's a subject I do know something about, paper. I wondered whether the Doctor ought to see it. Perhaps you can tell us.'

I examined the slip. It was nibbled all round the edges like any piece of paper would be that had been part of a mouse's nest. But it was true: the paper itself was of a special kind. It was real parchment. Then I read the few words which were written in four lines across the scrap of parchment.

Well, after that I decided that the Doctor ought to see it. And without further ado I took it to him and told him so.

Matthew happened to be with him in the study at the time. And in spite of the fact that he couldn't read, he became quite interested as soon as he heard where the paper had come from.

'But what made the mouse think it would be of importance?' asked the Doctor, as he took it from me and put on his spectacles.

'On account of the nature of the paper,' I said. 'It's real parchment, the kind they use for special legal documents.'

While the Doctor was reading the few words written on the torn scrap I watched his face carefully. And I felt sure from his expression that he guessed what I had guessed. But he evidently wasn't going to admit it. Rather hurriedly he handed it back to me.

'Yes, er – quite interesting, Stubbins,' he said, moving away from me. 'I'm rather busy just now. You'll excuse me, won't you?'

This was his polite way of telling me to go away and not bother him. And in the circumstances I felt there wasn't anything else to do but go.

Matthew's interest, on the other hand, was growing and as I left the room he followed me out. 'What do you make of that, Tommy?' he asked as soon as we had closed the door behind us.

'Why, between ourselves, Matthew,' I said, 'I think it's a will – or rather a piece of one. What's more, I believe the Doctor thinks so, too. But it is quite clear that he doesn't want to have anything to do with it. And nobody can blame him, after all he had to put up with from that horrible man.'

'A will?' said Matthew. 'Whose will?'

'We don't know,' I said 'This is all we have, just a corner of it.'

'A will, eh?' he muttered again. 'I wonder where that would fit in . . . Humph!'

'What do you mean, fit in?' I asked.

'Into the puzzle,' he said, staring at the floor lost in thought.

'I don't understand you, Matthew,' I said. 'What puzzle?'

'I'll tell you later,' he said, 'after I've found out a little more. But I knew I was right. There *was* a mystery in that house. Keep that piece of paper carefully.'

And at that he left me, with the scrap of parchment in my hand, pondering over his words.

7. The Mystery of Moorsden Manor

It was not long after this that Whitey came to me demanding to know what the Doctor had said about the scrap of torn parchment. I had to disappoint him by telling him that he had refused to show any interest in it whatever.

Jip was in my room at the time that Whitey stopped by. He had never quite forgiven me for having him sent back home the night of the fire – especially after he had learned later that there had been a fight and that his beloved Doctor had been treated so rudely by Throgmorton.

It was after supper, about half-past eight. And while Whitey and I were talking the Cats'-

meat-man also dropped in. I had not seen him for several days.

'Well, Matthew,' I said, 'how are you getting on with your mystery?'

'Humph!' he muttered, sinking into an armchair. 'It's still a mystery all right.'

Jip cocked up his ears at that and wanted to know what we were talking about. I explained to him, in dog language, that Matthew Mugg was sure that there was some mystery connected with the Manor and its owner.

'Tommy,' said Matthew, 'I can't make any more progress until we find the rest of that will.'

'I'm afraid that may be hard,' I said, 'from the inquiries I've made.'

'Listen,' Whitey whispered to me: 'I can get that mouse from the Manor for you any time you want.'

'All right,' I said. 'Send for him, will you, please? Maybe he's found out something since.'

Whitey disappeared and Matthew and I continued our conversation.

But it was less than quarter of an hour before Whitey was back at my elbow again. And with him he had the mouse who had brought us the scrap of parchment.

'Tell me,' I said to the Manor mouse, 'did you ever find out anything more about the rest of that paper?'

'As it happens,' he said, 'I did – tonight. The scrap, as I told you, had been in a mouse nest – an old one which I had discovered by accident and taken to pieces. You see, I was going to rebuild it into a new one for myself. Well, this evening I met the owner of that old nest.'

'Ah!' I said. 'That sounds like news. And what did he tell you?'

'It seems that it was in the days of this Mr Throgmorton's father when, he told me, he had lived in the old man's study on the first floor. He was building a nest for himself and his wife, and he made it behind the panelling – between the panelling and the wall. Nesting materials were hard to find. And he got into old Mr Throgmorton's desk – by drilling a hole through the back – and went through all the drawers looking for stuff he could use to make a nest of. Papers and red tape were about all he could find. And among the papers he chewed corners off, there was this large sheet which the old man kept locked up in the top drawer. My friend used it as a foundation for his nest because he saw it was nice and thick and would keep the draughts out.

'It seems the old man considered the paper important, because when, a few days later, he opened the drawer and found the corner chewed off, he swore and carried on something dreadful. The mouse was watching from behind the clock on the mantelpiece, and he says he never saw anyone get so angry. The old man saw right away that it was the work of mice, from the way in which the paper was nibbled. He hunted high and low for that missing corner – turned all the furniture in the whole room inside out. But of course he didn't find it because it was behind the panelling in my friend's nest. At last he gave it up and took the larger piece of the parchment away and hid it somewhere else.'

'Where?' I asked, rising half out of my chair.

'The old mouse said he didn't know. But wherever it was, it wasn't in the study.'

I sank back disappointed.

'Do you think,' I asked, 'that if all the mice

in the house went to work on it they could find it for us?'

The Manor mouse shook his head.

'As a matter of fact,' he said, 'we have tried. As soon as we learned that you were interested in the paper we began a search on our own. But we couldn't find a trace of it.'

I translated for Matthew's benefit what the Manor mouse had said, and his disappointment was even greater than mine.

'But tell me, Matthew,' I said, 'didn't you succeed in finding anything out yourself? Last time I saw you you were doing some investigating on your own.'

'It wasn't so easy,' he said, 'because when the old man died and this Mr Throgmorton came into the property, all the servants were changed. That's suspicious in itself, of course. So trying to find out much about the family from gossip was very hard.'

At this point Jip came up to my chair and nudged my knee beneath the table.

'Tommy,' he said. 'Cheapside the sparrow and I think we might be able to help. Cheapside's in touch with all the street sparrows and gets the gossip from them, which might be useful. And, well, I've often fancied myself as a dog detective so perhaps we could shed some light on the situation.'

8. The Dog Detective

So Cheapside, who had called that morning to visit the Doctor, was brought in from the garden, and the four of us went through the evidence again.

'Well,' said Jip, the Dog Detective, 'I think the first thing we should do is build up a story. In other words, try to solve it before we begin, by guesswork. Then we can go to work and see if we are right or not. Tell me, when you finally found Mr Throgmorton – or rather when he found you – did he have anything with him?'

'Yes,' I said, 'some small leather boxes.'

'Did you by any chance find out what they contained?'

'Yes,' I said again. 'Matthew opened one when Throgmorton wasn't looking. It had four large diamond studs in it.'

Jip nodded thoughtfully.

'And those two ferocious watch-dogs,' he went on, 'weren't they usually kept inside the house? Perhaps Matthew knows.'

I questioned the Cats'-meat-man.

'Yes,' he said. 'And that's still another thing I hadn't thought of before. The dogs were always brought into the house after dark and left loose to roam around. Yes, it was strange that that night Dina and Wolf were not inside the house at all. They were being kept by someone. It seemed as though they came from the stable.'

I interpreted to Jip. And he nodded again as though it all fitted in with his picture.

'Well, then,' he said, after a moment's thought, 'let us begin and build. Perhaps for the benefit of Matthew you had better explain to him once in a while what I am saying, so we can see whether he agrees with it or not. We will start off by supposing that since Mr Throgmorton was so annoyed with you – you who came to put the fire out – that he lighted it himself.'

I jumped slightly. It was such a startling idea.

'Just a minute, Jip,' I said. 'I'll put that to Matthew.

When I told Matthew, he jumped as well. 'Why that's an idea,' he said. 'An idea and a half, by Jiminy! And yet it fits in with some things, all right. I'd been thinking all the time that he was trying to get us off the place because he was doing something up there he hadn't oughter. I never thought of his setting fire to his own mansion – must be worth millions of pounds, that place, with all the stuff in it. And then he kicked up a fuss because we'd broken the windows. That don't sound as though he didn't care about the house . . . Just the same, it's an idea worth following up. Tell the dog to go on.'

'You see,' Jip continued, 'the fact that Sidney Throgmorton had his jewellery with him, also that this was the only night that the dogs were not kept in the house, makes it look as though he expected the fire.'

'Yes,' I said, 'that's right. But his loss would have been enormous just the same.'

'Wait,' said Jip. 'Maybe we'll find that his loss would have been even bigger if he didn't have the fire . . . Well, now, having supposed that Throgmorton set fire to his own house – it has been done before – the next question is: what did he want to burn it down for? He wanted to get rid of something, we'll say. What did he want to get rid of? Had he any people in it he wanted to kill?'

I questioned Matthew but there weren't any that he knew of.

'Any brothers or sisters?' asked Jip.

'None,' said Matthew. 'That I know for sure.'

'Very well,' Jip went on, 'then he wanted to destroy something, since people are out of the question. Why didn't he find the thing and get rid of it, instead of burning down a valuable house? Because he had tried and couldn't find it? Possibly. And almost certainly, if it was–'

'A will?' I broke in

'Exactly,' said Jip, nodding. 'Yet why destroy a will? Because in it he knew, or guessed, that his father had left the property not to him, the son, but to someone else. If there was no will he would get all the property because he was the only child. So, guessing there had been a will made; almost certain it was in that house; unable to find it himself, but terrified that someone else might – don't forget that he got rid of all the old servants and bought two ferocious watch-dogs to keep people out – finally he decides to burn the whole place down and the will with it. What does that loss matter when he had a dozen other houses and estates – which he never visited because he was afraid to leave the Manor in case someone found the will while he was away.'

9. A Friend to the Animals

'It fits, it fits!' cried Matthew, jumping up in excitement when I had explained what Jip had said. 'The gardener told me the father and son could never get along together. And that's why Sidney Throgmorton stayed abroad most of the time till after the old man died. And the father didn't want it known that they couldn't agree, see? So of course he would keep the will hidden. It all fits like a glove. The dog's a wizard. But listen: we ought to do something quickly. That man might try to burn the house down again any minute.'

One would have thought, to hear Matthew talk, that it was he who would lose most by the will's destruction. And I must confess that the fascination of the mystery had me in its grip by this time as well.

'Oh, I don't think he'll make another attempt in a hurry,' I said. 'It would look fishy. After all, he has got to be careful, you see. If he knows there was a will, then what he tried to do was a criminal offence – goodness, no wonder he was furious with us.'

'I reckon the next step,' said Jip, 'is to try and find out to whom the old Throgmorton would have been most likely to leave his money.'

At that, Cheapside, whom we had forgotten all about, hopped on to the table and started talking.

'Folks,' he said, 'I think I can help you there. I saw a good deal of the old Mr Throgmorton, and a mighty fine gentleman he was. It wasn't at Moorsden Manor that I saw him, because he only spent a week or two out of every year here. But at one of his other castles down in Sussex, where I used to go regular at one time in the early autumn. The old man retired from business when he was getting on in years and he spent his old age raising prize cows, sheep and horses. He was good to animals all round, was old

Jonathan T. Throgmorton. He had bird-fountains put out in all his gardens, nesting-boxes in the trees and everything. And he gave one of his footmen the special job of throwing out crumbs every morning for the sparrows and wild birds. Some days, when the old man was well enough, he used to do it himself. That's how I came to know him. Besides all that, he did a whole lot towards making life easier for other animals – paid to have drinking-troughs put up for horses, rescued stray dogs and even banned fox-hunting on his land. He was a friend to animals and a fine old gent, if ever there was one. I shouldn't wonder, Tommy, if he left part of his fortune to the same cause, the happiness of animals.'

Before Cheapside had quite finished speaking I got out the scrap of parchment which I had carefully kept in my pocket. I spread it out and re-read the few words which had been nibbled from the will. They were in four lines. The first line read: 'trustees who shall have–'. The second line, beginning a new paragraph, was: 'I bequeath–' The third: 'by said party or parties–' And the last: 'an Association for the Pre–'

To everyone's astonishment I suddenly sprang up and said: 'Let's all go and see the Doctor – as quickly as we can.'

The Manor mouse excused himself, saying that he ought to be getting back home as it was late and his wife might be worried. As we left the room Whitey told me he would accompany his friend as far as the gate and would join me in a minute or two in the Doctor's study. Together the rest of us, Matthew, Jip, Cheapside and I, went at once to the study, where we found John Dolittle, as usual, at work on his books.

'Doctor,' I cried, bursting in, 'I'm dreadfully sorry to interrupt you, but I really feel you ought to hear this.'

With a patient sigh he laid down his pen as I told him the story.

'Now, don't you see, Doctor,' I ended, showing him the scrap of parchment again, 'it is practically certain that when this piece is joined to the rest that last line will read, "an Association for the Prevention of Cruelty to Animals", or some such title. For that is the cause in which this man had already spent great sums of money while he was alive. And that is the cause which his horrible son Sidney Throgmorton has probably robbed of a large fortune. Doctor, it is the animals who have been cheated.'

We all watched the Doctor's face eagerly as he thought for a silent moment about what I had just said. After a while I thought I saw signs of agreement in his face.

'But, Stubbins,' he said quietly, 'aren't you basing most of this on guesswork, though I admit it sounds believable. Tell me: what do you want me to do?'

'Doctor,' I said, 'we've got to get that will.'

'Yes, yes, I see that,' he said. 'But how? Even if we got into the house – risking arrest for burglary and all that – what chance would we stand of finding it, if Sidney Throgmorton, living there all the time and hunting for it ever since his father's death, couldn't find it?'

I saw at once that he was right. The difficulties of what I had suggested were enormous. But while I stood there, silent and confused, I suddenly heard Whitey out in the passage squeaking at the top of his voice: 'Tommy! Tommy! They've found it. They've found it! The mice have found the will!'

10. *The Secret Cupboard*

Whitey was so breathless with running when he appeared at the study door that he could hardly talk. I lifted him to the table, where between puffs he finally managed to give us this message.

Apparently, just as he was seeing the Manor mouse off at the gate, a rat had run up and said that they had at last found the document. The old man had hidden it, it seemed, in a secret cupboard on the top floor of the house. They couldn't get the will out because it was a large heavy roll of parchment; and the hole which they had made into the cupboard (through the brickwork at the back) was very, very small.

Indeed, it was so tiny that the two rats who had made it couldn't get through it. But they could see that there were papers of some sort inside. So they had got the very smallest mouse in the Manor and sent him in to make an examination and give them a report. And they were now quite certain that the document was the will, because it was made of the same kind of parchment and had a corner missing just like the one which I had.

Well, as you can imagine, the excitement among us was tremendous. And when, a moment later, the rat in question himself appeared, confirmed the story, and offered to lead the Doctor at once to the secret cupboard, I could see that the thrill of the Moorsden Manor Mystery was beginning to take hold of John Dolittle himself.

Matthew was all for starting right away.

'No, now wait a minute,' said the Doctor. 'Not so fast. This is a serious thing. If we should be wrong and get caught we will have hard work to explain our actions – especially with Sidney Throgmorton anxious to put us all in jail, anyway. We must be very careful and make as few mistakes as possible. Let me see: what time is it? Eleven forty-five. We couldn't attempt it before two o'clock in the morning, anyhow. We must be sure everyone's in bed first. Listen, Jip: you run over there to the Manor. Could you get into the grounds, do you think?

'Oh, yes,' said Jip. 'I can slip through the bars of that big gate easily.'

'Well,' said the Doctor, 'don't be seen, for Heaven's sake. They might shoot you. Then just nose quietly round the house till you get a chance to speak to those two watch-dogs, Dina and Wolf. Tell them to expect me about two o'clock and not to be worried or give any alarm if they hear latches being forced or anything like that. Do you understand?'

'All right,' said Jip. And he hopped through the open window into the darkness of the garden and was gone.

'Now, the next thing we'll need,' said the Doctor, 'is a rope. See if you can find one up in the attic please, Stubbins.'

'Will we be taking Bumpo along, Doctor?' asked Matthew. 'Better, don't you think? He's a handy man in a tight place.'

'Er – yes, I suppose so,' said John Dolittle.

'Then I'll go and start getting him woke up,' said the Cats'-meat-man. 'It's a long job as a rule.'

Well although we had two and a quarter hours in which to make our preparations it didn't seem too long. One after another we'd all think of things we ought to take, or do, to ensure success to the expedition. And when John Dolittle finally looked at his watch and said that we ought to be starting, it didn't seem more than a few minutes since he had made up his mind to set off on this adventure.

Fortunately there would be no moon until about three o'clock in the morning. So to begin with we had the protection of complete darkness.

Despite the fact that I shared Polynesia's confidence in the Doctor's luck and success, I must confess I felt quite scared by the risks ahead of us as we quietly opened the gate and trailed down to the road.

The Doctor and Matthew had worked out our plan before we left and had given us our roles so there was no talking as we plodded along the road to the Manor.

At a point where the branch of a large tree overhung the high wall of the estate we stopped and the Doctor uncoiled his rope. With the aid of a stone tied to a long length of twine, we got the rope's end hauled up over the branch and down to the road again. Up this we all swarmed in turn.

Meanwhile Cheapside kept watch in the branches above to see that no one surprised us. When we were all inside the grounds, we hauled the rope after us.

When I got down out of the tree the first thing I noticed was Jip's white shadow flitting across the lawn.

'It's all right,' he whispered to the Doctor. 'I've told Dina and Wolf. They say they will be on the look out for you and will show you round the place when you get in.'

'Yes, but it is *getting in* that is going to be the job, I'm afraid,' muttered John Dolittle. 'Listen, Jip: from here I've no idea of even where the house lies – through all these trees and bushes. 'Lead us to it please, Jip.'

'Very well,' said Jip. 'I'll take you to the

kitchen-garden side. You'll have cover all the way. But if you should get spotted and have to run for it, tell everyone to follow me. I know the easiest and shortest way out.'

Then in single file we followed Jip, who kept us behind bushes and hedges for what seemed like a good ten minutes' walk. Suddenly we found ourselves against the wall of the house itself.

'Listen,' Jip whispered to the Doctor, 'you've got that rat in your pocket still, haven't you – the one who lives here?'

'Yes,' said John Dolittle. 'And Whitey, too,'

'Well, that rat is your best chance for getting in,' said Jip. 'If you let Matthew force a lock you're liable to have complications with the police afterwards. Send the rat into the house through a hole – he'll know lots of them leading down into the cellar. And tell him to get you the master's front-door key. It'll be in his bedroom, on the dressing-table – they usually are.'

'Splendid!' whispered the Doctor. And at once he took the rat from his pocket and explained to him what Jip had said. Then he let him go upon the ground and we waited.

It was about five minutes later, I should say, when I felt something small and sharp hit me on the head. Even through my cap it stung. From my head it bounced to the ground. And by the dim starlight I could see it shining dully where it lay. I picked it up. It was a small key.

Apparently the master's bedroom was directly above our heads; and the rat, to save time, had thrown the key out of the window.

I slipped it into the Doctor's hand and in silence we moved round towards the front of the house.

11. Whitey to the Rescue

It had been agreed that only Matthew would
accompany the Doctor to the top floor. I was
to wait downstairs in the hall, and Bumpo was to
stay outside the house. His and my parts in the
plot were mostly those of watching and standing
on guard. In case of emergency we had signals
arranged and were to meet at a certain point.

As the Doctor very, very quietly opened the
front door I got my first real scare of the
evening. With frightening suddenness, both
together, the two ferocious heads of the watch-
dogs popped out to greet him.

Within the hall, where the darkness was
quite intense, I confess that I was quite glad that

I wasn't going any farther. As we had arranged, I sat down on the floor by the front door and began my watch. Jip, thank goodness, stayed with me. Matthew and the Doctor, each with a hand on the collar of one of the guiding watch-dogs, were led away swiftly and silently through the inky blackness, up carpeted stairs, to the room above.

They seemed to be gone for ages. Every time the breeze rattled a window or swung a curtain whispering across the floor, I was convinced that we had been discovered and someone was coming after us. It was a great temptation to open the front door and let in the little light of the starry sky outside. But I had been told to keep it closed in case the draught was noticed by someone in the house.

At last Jip whispered: 'Don't get scared now if someone bumps into you. They're coming down the stairs again. I can smell 'em.'

A moment later the wet muzzle of Dina, leading the Doctor across the hall, dabbed me in the ear. It was a good thing Jip had warned me – I should probably have started hitting out in all directions if he hadn't. I rose and carefully swung open the front door. The dim forms of the Doctor and Matthew passed out. I followed. With a pat of thanks John Dolittle turned and shut the two dogs in behind us, and locked the door. Then he took the rat from his pocket, gave him the key and put him on the ground. From somewhere out of the general gloom of the garden, Bumpo's huge figure emerged and joined us.

Once more under Jip's guidance we began the journey across the park towards the walls. I was simply burning up to ask the Doctor if he had succeeded, but I managed to restrain my curiosity till we stood beneath the large tree. Then at last I whispered: 'Did you get it?'

'Yes,' he said. 'It's in my pocket. Everything went fine. We were able to open the cupboard and close it again too, leaving it so no one would know we were there. But, of course, I haven't had a chance to read the will yet. Come along now, where's that rope?'

Again, one by one, we swarmed to the top of the wall, transferred the dangling rope to the other side and slid quietly down into the road.

With a general sigh we set off towards home. As we passed the gate we noticed the grey of the dawn showing in the east. Like a silent ghost Jip slipped out through the bars and dropped in behind the procession.

On reaching the house we all hurried to the study. I got some candles lighted while the Doctor spread the will out on the table. It was a tense moment for all of us as we leaned over his shoulder.

Sure enough, a piece had been bitten out of the document at the corner. And when I added the fragment I had in my pocket it fitted perfectly. Then, without going through the beginning, the Doctor traced that paragraph with his finger. This is what he read out: 'I bequeath the sum of one hundred thousand pounds for the endowment of an Association for the Prevention of Cruelty to Animals. The Trustees will select–'

But he didn't get any further. Matthew, Bumpo and I suddenly started cheering and dancing round the table. And it was quite some minutes before our enthusiasm had let off enough steam to allow us to listen to any more.

As we settled down into our chairs again I noticed the Doctor staring at something

Matthew was turning over in his fingers. I started as I saw what it was – one of the diamond shirt-studs from Sidney Throgmorton's little leather box.

'Er – where – did you get that, Matthew?' asked the Doctor, in a low, rather fearful voice.

'Oh, this?' said the Cats'-meat-man, trying hard not to look guilty. 'This is a little souvenir I brought along from the Manor.'

For a moment the Doctor seemed too horrified to speak.

'Well,' Matthew went on, 'it wasn't his, you know, after all, with him robbing the animals of that whole fortune what was coming to them according to the will.'

'But when, how, did you take it, Matthew?' asked the Doctor. 'I thought you were with me all the time.'

'Oh, I just dropped into his bedroom to take a look around, as we passed his door going up the stairs,' said Matthew. 'These pretty playthings was in a box on the dressing-table, and I couldn't resist the temptation of bringing one along as a souvenir.'

With his hand to his head the Doctor sank into a chair as if stunned.

'Oh, Matthew, Matthew!' he murmured. 'I thought you had promised me to give up that sort of thing for good.'

For a moment we were all silent. Finally the Doctor said: 'Well, I don't know what we are to do now, really I don't.'

Whitey crawled up my sleeve from the table and whispered in my ear: 'What's the matter with the Doctor? What has happened?'

I explained to him as quickly and as briefly as I could.

'Give me that stud, Doctor,' he said, suddenly darting across the table to John Dolittle. 'I'll get it back into its box before you can say Jack Robinson.'

'Goodness! Do you think you could?' cried the Doctor, immediately all cheered up. 'Oh, but look: the daylight is here now. The disappearance of the diamond has probably already been noticed. And think of the time it would take you to travel there – at your pace!'

'Doctor, it wouldn't take long if he rode on my back,' Jip put in. 'If I carry him as far as the house he can soon pop in through a hole and slip upstairs. It's worth trying.'

'All right,' said the Doctor, 'good idea.'

And to Matthew's great disappointment he leaned across the table, took the valuable jewel out of his hands and gave it to Whitey.

'You'll save us from a terrible mess,' he said, 'if you can get it there in time. Good luck to you!'

Whitey took the stud in his paws, jumped on to Jip's back and disappeared through the garden window at a gallop.

After he had gone there was an embarrassed, uncomfortable pause. Finally the Doctor said: 'Er – Stubbins and Bumpo: you will not of course mention this matter to a living soul.'

Feeling very uncomfortable, we nodded in silence.

'As for you, Matthew,' the Doctor went on,

'I must warn you now, once and for all, that if any other occurrence of this sort takes place we shall have to stop being friends. I know I can trust you with my own possessions but I must feel secure that you will treat the possessions of others in the same way. If not, we can have nothing further to do with one another. Do you understand?'

'Yes, I understand, Doctor,' said Matthew in a low voice. 'I ought to have known I might be putting you in an awkward situation. But – well, no more need be said.'

The Doctor turned as though to go into the garden. He looked about him for his hat. And suddenly a look of horror came slowly onto his face.

'Stubbins!' he gasped. 'Where is it?'

'Don't tell me,' I cried, 'that you left it again – *in the Manor.*'

12. Our Arrest

It was true. In the thrill and excitement of our night time adventure none of us had noticed whether the Doctor had come away from the Manor with his hat on or not. But now that we came to think of it we all remembered him wearing it on the way there. Next, he himself remembered clearly that in getting into the secret cupboard he had put it on a chair because it was in the way.

'Dear me!' he sighed, shaking his head. 'That's the kind of a burglar I am – leave my hat behind me, the one thing that everybody in the neighbourhood would recognize as mine . . . Hah! It would be funny if it wasn't so serious.

Well, more than ever depends on Whitey now. Dear, dear! Anyhow,' he added as Dab-Dab appeared at the door, 'let's not meet our troubles halfway. Breakfast ready, Dab-Dab?'

'No,' said the housekeeper, coming forward into the room and lowering her voice. 'But there are three men walking up the garden path. One is carrying your hat. And one is a policeman.'

At that Matthew sprang up and in a twinkling was half out of the garden window. Then, apparently changing his mind, he stopped.

'No, Doctor,' he said, coming back into the room, 'I ain't going to leave you to face the music. I'll tell them *I* did it.'

'Look here, Matthew,' said John Dolittle firmly: 'I want you to do one thing only throughout the rest of this business, and that is keep your mouth closed tight – unless I ask you to talk. Stubbins, will you please let them in?'

I went and opened the door. I knew all three men by sight. One was Sidney Throgmorton; the other his lodge-keeper; and the third our local police sergeant. The sergeant's manner was very apologetic. He knew John Dolittle, and this duty was distasteful to him. Throgmorton's behaviour, on the other hand, was offensive from the start. He brushed by me before I had invited him to come in and walked straight to the Doctor's study.

'Ah!' he cried. 'We have the whole lot here, Sergeant – the same party exactly that came pretending to put the fire out when they wanted to learn their way around the house they meant later to rob. Put them all under arrest and bring them at once to the Manor.'

The sergeant, while he was somewhat impressed by Throgmorton's position in the community, knew what his duties were without being told. He addressed himself to John Dolittle.

'This gentleman has brought a charge, Doctor,' he said. 'A valuable diamond was stolen from his house last night and your hat was found on the premises this morning. I shall have to ask you to come up to the Manor, please.'

We were all glad that it was so early in the morning because that meant the streets were empty as we were marched up to the Manor. For certainly our group with the sergeant for escort would have set gossip running all over Puddleby if there had been anyone awake to see us.

At the house the old servant let us in and we went straight upstairs to the master's bedroom. Here Throgmorton at once plunged into a dramatic story, for the sergeant's benefit, of how he had woken up as usual at six o'clock and had noticed at once that his stud-box had been moved from the place where it stood the night before. He opened it, he said, and found one stud missing. After the servants had been summoned and a search made of the house, the Doctor's hat had been found in a room on the top floor. This, and the fact that we had all behaved in a suspicious manner the night of the fire, made us guilty in his mind.

'Just a minute,' said the Doctor. 'Is the box now in the exact place where you found it when you got up?'

'Yes,' said Throgmorton.

'Well, would you show us, please, just how you went to the dressing-table and opened it?'

'Certainly,' said Throgmorton. 'I walked from the bed, like this, and first opened the curtains at the window, so. Then one glance at the dressing-table told me something was wrong. I stepped up to it – so – lifted the box and opened it. Like this . . . What the–'

At that last exclamation of astonishment we all four breathed a secret sigh of relief. For it told us that Whitey had done his work. I shall never forget Throgmorton's face as he stood there, staring in the box. In it there were not three studs, as he had expected, but the complete set of four.

The sergeant looked over his shoulder.

'There's been some mistake, sir, hasn't there?' he said quietly.

'There's b–b–b–been some trickery,' cried Throgmorton, spluttering. Indeed his anger and confusion were understandable in the circumstances. He would much rather have got John Dolittle into jail than recovered his stud. And this small quiet man seemed to have a knack for making a fool of him at the most dramatic moments.

'If you didn't do it,' he snarled, swinging round on the Doctor and pointing a fat accusing finger at him, 'how did your hat come to be in my house?'

'I think,' said the Doctor, 'it would be best if I gave you an answer to that question in private.'

'No,' snapped Throgmorton. 'If it's the truth there's no harm in the police sergeant hearing it.'

'As you wish,' said the Doctor. 'But I thought you would prefer it that way. It has to do with a will whose existence we discovered by accident.'

Astonishment, fear and hatred flitted across Throgmorton's face before he answered.

'All right,' he said sullenly at last. 'We will go down to the library.'

In a silent, very thoughtful procession we returned down the several flights of stairs. At the tail of it came Matthew and myself.

'Thank goodness for Whitey and Jip!' he whispered in my ear. 'But I don't like trusting that fellow alone with the Doctor.'

'Don't worry,' I replied. 'We'll be outside the door. He wouldn't dare start any violence with the sergeant here as a witness. His game's up.'

I heard the big grandfather clock in the hall strike as the Doctor and Throgmorton went into the library and closed the door behind them. And it was exactly three-quarters of an hour before they came out.

Throgmorton was very white, but quite

quiet. He immediately spoke to the policeman.

'The charge is withdrawn, sergeant,' he said. 'A mistake – for which I must apologise to – er – all concerned. I'm sorry I got you up here so early when there was no need.'

Again in silence we trailed across the wide carpeted hall and out into the gravel court.

At the gate we said goodbye to the sergeant, who was going in a different direction. I noticed that the Doctor made no comment about the whole episode to him.

When he was well out of earshot Matthew asked eagerly: 'But, Doctor, how did you explain your hat being there?'

'I didn't,' said John Dolittle. 'But I told him that all of us were convinced he lit that fire and that I could prove it. Which I can't. But it is just as well that he thinks so, because I feel sure he did. He is going back to Australia now.'

'To Australia!' cried Matthew. 'Why?'

'Well he has to earn a living, you see,' said the Doctor. 'The will left not only the one hundred thousand pounds for the prevention of cruelty to animals, but when I came to read it through I found that it left the rest to other charities.'

13. Celebrations

When the outcome of the Moorsden Manor mystery became generally known in the Dolittle household, celebrations broke out and lasted for two days. But Whitey said that since animals in general had come into a considerable fortune thanks to the Doctor, the celebrations should be open to all animals. So he got the Doctor's permission and sent out an invitation to all the creatures in the neighbourhood who wanted to come. An enormous amount of preparation was made. The house was decorated with ribbons and streamers by day and with lanterns and fireworks at night. All sorts of good things to eat and drink were bought and set out for all the animals.

The crowd that came was much bigger than we'd expected. Gub-Gub, Whitey, Chee-Chee, Too-Too, Dab-Dab and Polynesia worked hard to feed and entertain everyone.

As for the Doctor, Matthew, Bumpo and me, we were kept busy running between the house and the town for more and more food. Too-Too, the accountant, told me afterwards that according to his books we had bought more than a wagon-load of lettuces, three hundred-weight of corn and birdseed, close on a ton of bones and meat, four large cheeses and two dozen loaves – besides a great number of delicacies in smaller quantity.

In the Doctor's garden it was almost impossible to move along the lawns, so full were they with hedgehogs, moles, squirrels, stoats, rats, badgers, mice, voles, otters, hares and what not. The animals danced and at frequent intervals cheers for the Doctor, old Mr Throgmorton, or his Association for the Prevention of Cruelty to Animals, would break out in some corner and be quickly taken up by everyone else. Every tree and bush in the garden was packed with perching birds of all kinds and sizes, from wrens to herons. The din of their chatter was constant and terrific.

Before the day was over the grass of the garden was worn away by all those millions of feet. And after the guests had left, it took the members of Doctor Dolittle's animal family another whole day to clear away the scraps and put the place in order.

But as the last feeding trough had been cleared away and the last lantern taken down from the shrubbery, we all trooped back into the house and slumped exhausted in front of the big fire which Dab-Dab had started in the hearth.

Through the flickering flames I watched the Doctor take off his hat and rub his tired eyes.

'Well,' I said, 'we've had quite an adventure.'

'And it's all thanks to the Doctor that everything's worked out so well,' said Matthew, balancing a mug of cocoa on his knee.

'Yes, Doctor,' I said. 'You really did save the day this time.'

'I'll drink to that,' said the Cats'-meat-man, and we all raised our mugs as the Doctor smiled a very contented smile.